Hybrids

Angela Hunt

Alton Gansky, Bill Myers,
and Frank Peretti

D1264641

Published by Amaris Media International.
Copyright © 2016 Angela Hunt
Cover Design: Angela Hunt
Photos ©BestPhotoStudio *fotolia.com.*

ISBN 13: 978-0692638538
ISBN-10: 0692638539

For more information, visit us on Facebook:
https://www.facebook.com/pages/Harbingers/705107309586877

or *www.harbingersseries.com.*

HARBINGERS

A novella series by
Bill Myers, Frank Peretti, Angela Hunt, and Alton
Gansky

In this fast-paced world with all its demands, the four of us wanted to try something new. Instead of the longer novel format, we wanted to write something equally as engaging but that could be read in one or two sittings—on the plane, waiting to pick up the kids from soccer, or as an evening's read.

We also wanted to play. As friends and seasoned novelists, we thought it would be fun to create a game we could participate in together. The rules were simple:

Rule #1

Each of us would write as if we were one of the characters in the series:

Bill Myers would write as Brenda, the street-hustling tattoo artist who sees images of the future.

Frank Peretti would write as the professor, the atheist ex-priest ruled by logic.

Angela Hunt would write as Andi, the professor's brilliant-but-geeky assistant who sees inexplicable patterns.

Alton Gansky would write as Tank, the naïve, big-hearted jock with a surprising connection to a healing power.

Rule #2

Instead of the four of us writing one novella together (we're friends but not crazy), we would write it like a TV series. There would be an overarching story line into which we'd plug our individual novellas, with each story written from our character's point of view.

If you're keeping track, this is the order:

Harbingers #1—*The Call*—Bill Myers
Harbingers #2—*The Haunted*—Frank Peretti
Harbingers #3—*The Sentinels*—Angela Hunt
Harbingers #4—*The Girl*—Alton Gansky

Volumes #1-4 omnibus: *Cycle One: Invitation*

Harbingers #5—*The Revealing*—Bill Myers
Harbingers #6—*Infestation*—Frank Peretti
Harbingers #7—*Infiltration*—Angela Hunt
Harbingers #8—*The Fog*—Alton Gansky

Volumes #5-8 omnibus: *Cycle Two: Mosaic*

Harbingers #9—*Leviathan*—Bill Myers
Harbingers #10—*The Mind Pirates*—Frank Peretti
Harbingers #11—*Hybrids*—Angela Hunt
Harbingers #12—*The Village*—Alton Gansky

There you have it—at least for now. We hope you'll find these as entertaining in the reading as we are in the writing.

Bill, Frank, Angie, and Al

Chapter 1

I stood at the bottom of the Tampa airport's escalator and searched for Tank with an odd mingling of excitement and dread. Excitement, because I hadn't seen him, Brenda, or Daniel in several weeks, not since we parted after our adventure in the Caribbean. Dread, because each time I met Tank after a separation, his face lit up like Times Square on New Year's and I didn't know what to do about that. I loved him like a brother, but clearly, he felt something more for me . . . feelings I didn't think I could ever reciprocate.

I blew out a breath and studied the passengers on the escalator. Most wore the look of people who'd spent too much time in a cramped space, but a few faces were smiling, probably because they were meeting the pretty young women who held welcome signs for the various cruise lines. Tampa was a major

port, and who wouldn't look forward to a few days at sea? As long as we didn't encounter pirates, even I might be tempted to board a sailboat again.

"Andi!"

I smiled up at Tank, who seemed to span the entire width of the escalator as he waved. I pointed to the baggage carousel for his airline, then walked toward it. Tank was loud, enthusiastic, and eager— not exactly the sort of person I wanted to meet in front of all those people coming down the escalator.

I had no sooner arrived at the baggage area than I felt my feet leave the ground. Tank had come up from behind and wrapped me in a bear hug, and his overly rambunctious greeting lifted me at least two feet off the floor. "Andi, it's so good to see you," he said. "I didn't think we'd ever land."

"I'm glad you did. Now, will you please put me down?"

He lowered me gently, then stepped to my side, arms extended as if he planned to hug me again. I lifted my hand and patted his chest in an effort to hold him off. "Brenda and Daniel came in yesterday and spent today at Disney World. They'll probably be back around dinner time."

"Sure was nice of your grandparents to let us use their house again." Tank picked up the gym bag he'd dropped behind me. "After our last visit, I wasn't sure they'd want to have us again."

I smiled, not needing to be reminded of the last time we'd gathered at the beach house. In the space of a few days, we encountered dead fish and birds, alien creatures, and a green slime that ended up nearly killing me. I hoped *this* little vaycay would bring nothing but the rest and relaxation I'd promised the

4

others.

"How's the professor?" Tank asked.

I glanced up to see if he was asking out of concern or mere politeness, but honest curiosity shone from Tank's eyes. I had to admit—whatever else he was, Tank was a genuinely good guy. He cared about people, even the professor, who seemed to try everyone else's patience.

"He's good," I said, tempering my voice. "Working hard on a presentation he's supposed to deliver tomorrow at the University of Tampa."

Tank frowned. "What's wrong? Something's bothering you, I can tell."

I hesitated. I hadn't mentioned my concerns to Brenda because I didn't want to ruin her plans for Disney, *and* because I was hoping my worries were only the result of a hyperactive imagination. But I couldn't get anything by Tank . . .

"I'm a little worried about the professor, to tell you the truth. His paper is supposed to be on dimensionality and quantum mechanics, with an emphasis on multiple universes. He finished his first draft weeks ago, but he keeps muttering and tinkering with it—" I shrugged. "I don't know. He just seems . . . unsatisfied, and that's not like him."

"Ain't he a perfectionist?"

"He is . . . but this dissatisfaction seems different. I can't quite put my finger on why, but something's going on in his head, something he's not sharing with me. And that's not like him, either."

Tank's brow furrowed for a minute, then he grinned. "Don't worry. When the team is together, we always seem to figure things out." He draped his arm casually over my shoulder, then nodded to a bulky hard case coming down the conveyor belt. "That's my bag."

"Good grief." I gawked at the long case. "What is that, a trombone case?"

"Metal detector." Tank grinned. "I've heard that you can find a fortune on the beach—rings, coins, all kinds of stuff. Since we're just gonna be hangin' out at your grandparents' place, I thought I might pick up a new hobby."

I resisted the urge to roll my eyes. "Whatever. Grab your new toy and I'll meet you on the curb."

Brenda's rental car was parked in the driveway when Tank and I pulled up. Daniel bounded out of the house as I got out of the car. "Space Mountain!" he said, his eyes as wide as saucers. "And more pirates!"

Brenda grinned as she stepped onto the front porch. "I see you had no trouble finding the Tankster."

"Hard to miss him," I quipped, then I bent to Daniel's eye level. "I didn't expect to see you so soon. I thought you'd stay at the Magic Kingdom all day."

Brenda gave Tank a firm slug to the upper arm, then threw me a look. "Can you spell *overstimulation*? I figured we should leave before Daniel short-circuited. If the weather looks good and I can stretch my budget, maybe we'll go back another day this week. But we had a great time."

I glanced toward the front door. "Is the professor—?"

"Locked in his room." Brenda lifted a brow. "I don't know what he's doin' in there, but I can hear him muttering behind the door. Kinda creepy, if you want to know the truth. I know he tends to be anti-social, but today he's taking *grumpy* to a whole new level."

I sighed. "Let's all give him some space. I think he's worried about his presentation tomorrow. When it's over, he'll relax. Maybe."

I didn't tell her about my frustrations—about how he'd taken to locking himself in his office and he hadn't let me read his latest paper. I didn't want to invade his privacy and confess that I'd pressed my ear to his office door and heard him sobbing. Cursing, too, at times, and at least twice I'd heard the sound heavy objects being thrown across the room.

I thought the professor and I were close, but apparently we weren't close enough to share whatever secrets he'd been hiding. But how was I supposed to do my job if he closed himself off from me?

I opened the trunk looked around to make sure I hadn't forgotten anything as Tank had grabbed his bag and his metal detector and headed into the house. I turned to follow, but couldn't help noticing a pair of children on the sidewalk across the street. They appeared to be about nine or ten, and they were standing motionless, neither of them speaking. They were staring at me.

Something about them sent a chill up the ladder of my spine. I couldn't remember the last time I'd seen kids of that age who weren't fidgeting, running, or talking a mile a minute. We saw a lot of children on this street, most of them tourists whose families had come to enjoy Florida's sandy beaches. But I'd never seen any kids like these.

I stepped forward to study them more closely.

Something else about them seemed odd—their clothes. Most kids in the area wore tee shirts, baggy shorts, and flip flops or sneakers. These children were wearing long, dark pants, oversized long-sleeved shirts, and dark shoes. Like children from some reclusive sect that didn't believe in showing too much skin . . .

I lifted my chin, forced a smile, and twiddled my fingers at them, then turned and walked toward the front door. But before going inside, I threw a glance over my shoulder. The children had gone. Moved on, I supposed, to explore some other local resident.

And with their disappearance, I felt an overwhelming wave of relief.

Chapter 2

The kid from Perfect Pasta had just delivered orders of spaghetti, lasagna, and pepperoni pizza when I spotted my grandparents' neighbor, Mrs. Diaz, waddling toward our front door.

"Tank," I called, struggling to handle the bag of food and a large pizza box while Abby, my chocolate Lab, danced at my feet in anticipation of pasta. "Will you take these while I pay for this stuff?"

Tank came to my aid in a flash, and after paying the delivery dude, I walked to the edge of the porch to greet Mrs. Diaz.

"Andi, so good to see you." She smiled, then handed me a small package. "This was delivered to our house by mistake. I think it's your grandfather's medicine."

I checked the label—sure enough, the mail carrier had left it in the wrong box. "Very nice of you to bring it over, Mrs. Diaz. Especially—" I grinned— "in your condition."

"What are neighbors for?" She smiled, then rubbed her very pregnant belly. "The walking does me good. I'm trying to convince this baby to make an early appearance."

"When are you due?"

"Two more weeks." She gave me a rueful smile. "But he's strong and healthy, so he can come any time. Fine with me."

"I hope he comes soon, then. And I'll bet your husband is thrilled."

"He's always wanted a boy. Machismo, you know." She rolled her eyes, then turned toward her house. "Tell your grandparents I said hello."

"They're in New York for the week, but I'll tell them," I called. "And I hope that baby comes soon."

I went back inside the house, dropped Sabba's package onto the foyer table, then joined the others in the dining room. Tank, Brenda, Daniel, and even the professor had already gathered around the table. Brenda had taken charge, which was fine with me, and was passing out silverware, paper plates, and napkins. Daniel had sunk into the chair at the head of the table, leaving the professor to take the empty chair at the other end.

I smothered a smile. He might be nervous about his speech, but the professor was not so preoccupied that he'd let a ten-year-old challenge his right to sit at the head of the table.

"Sorry I'm late," I told them, dropping into an empty chair. "Let's eat."

"Just a minute." Tank bowed his head as he always did. "Lord, thanks for this food, and keep us safe during this time together. Amen."

The professor cleared his throat as we began to pass dishes and serve ourselves. "Before the conversation drifts into mundane topics, I'd like to welcome everyone. And while I certainly won't demand that you attend my lecture tomorrow, I thought you all might like to come—especially since we've had first-hand experience with other dimensions and universes."

"We'll be there," I said, shooting a sharp glance around the table in case anyone was thinking of sleeping in. "We'll be cheering you on."

"Thank you, Andi, but this group's quiet, polite, and discreet presence will be more than enough."

"Are you sure Daniel can handle it?" A line trenched the center of Brenda's forehead. "He's still a little amped up from seeing Mickey Mouse. That stuffy atmosphere might be too much for him."

"Nice try, Barnick, but you're not getting out of this one," the professor answered. "I think you might actually profit from learning a few things you obviously skipped in high school."

Brenda scowled at the professor, then grinned at me. "Actually, I skipped most of high school. And I get along just fine."

"Be that as it may," the professor continued, pressing his hands together, "I thought I might take a few minutes tonight to acquaint you with a few elementary principles so you won't be totally lost at the symposium."

"Professor, I'm not sure—" I began, but Tank cut me off.

"I'm listenin'," Tank said, one side of his mouth bulging with pizza. "I don't know nothin' about that stuff, but if you can help me look less like a fool, I'm up for it."

I picked up my fork and cut a bite of lasagna. If the others were willing to endure a lecture with their meal, how could I object?

"I know you understand the idea of three dimensions," the professor began. "Objects in our world—like that salt shaker there—have width, height, and breadth. A line, however, has only two dimensions—length and width."

"*Flatland*," Brenda said. "I don't remember much about high school, but I do remember that book. Everyone in the book was a line, and if you looked at them sideways, they were long. If you looked at them straight on, they looked like little dots." She snorted. "Crazy stuff."

"Um—yes. Exactly." The professor nodded. "Flatland was a two-dimensional world. We are most familiar with three dimensions."

"I remember something," Tank said. "I forget which movie it was, but Superman takes the bad guys and puts them in these flat things and spins them into space. They trapped and can't get out."

The professor gaze Tank a quizzical look—clearly, he wasn't a Superman fan—then sighed. "Actually, tomorrow I'll be talking about dimensions that exist beyond the three we know."

"Hang on." Brenda's dark eyes gleamed with interest. "Are you going to be talkin' about the beings Daniel can see? Angels and such?"

The professor shifted his gaze to Daniel, who was focused on plucking pepperonis from his pizza. "Not exactly. First, I'm going to discuss the fourth dimension, which is time. We are accustomed to living moment by moment, existing for a certain time in a certain place. But if you could exist in the fourth dimension of time, you might look like a long worm that snaked through all the spaces where you've ever spent even a single second. The worm would be small at one end, where you occupied a smaller space because you were a child, and it would grow to the size of your adult body until the place where your lifeline ends."

Tank sucked at the inside of his cheek for a moment, then shook his head. "Unless your lifeline doesn't end. Maybe it just transfers out of one dimension and moves to a higher one. Maybe it moves to a place where angels and demons live, or maybe it goes to a place even higher than that. You don't really know where a soul goes after death, do you? And you can't prove anything, because no one has really died—I mean, *really* died—and come back to tell us about it." A confident grin spread across his face. "Well, except for the one guy, but the professor doesn't wanna believe in Him."

The professor threw me a glance of helpless appeal, then sighed and picked up his fork. "I think I've prepared you enough," he said, sliding his fork into a mound of spaghetti. "Just remember—tomorrow's lecture is not a forum for discussion. If you have questions—" he glared at Tank—"keep them to yourself. We can talk about them at dinner tomorrow night."

I shot Tank a warning look—why was he trying to rattle the professor's cage on the night before his big speech?—but Tank only gave me a wide-eyed look of innocence as the professor spun spaghetti onto his fork.

Chapter 3

Tank stopped halfway into the row of padded seats and turned to me. "Are you sure they don't serve popcorn at these things?"

"I'm sure." I pushed him forward. "You're supposed to take notes, not feed your face. So keep moving, please."

Tank sighed heavily, but I had a feeling he was actually looking forward to the professor's presentation. Brenda and Daniel filed in after me, then we made ourselves comfortable in the big, comfy chairs of the university's auditorium.

I took advantage of the house lights and looked

around. Lots of scholarly-looking men and women in the audience, lots of jeans and elbow- patched jackets on people who looked as though they spent a lot of time reading. More men than women. Brenda and I actually stood out. So did Daniel.

Daniel pulled his iPhone out of his pocket and began to play one of his games. "Okay," Brenda said, "but you have to mute the sound."

Daniel grunted, then pressed the mute button and kept playing. Someone lowered the house lights and a hush fell over the crowd. An expectant atmosphere filled the room, the same sort of anticipation you might experience at a beauty pageant, a concert, or a play . . . except this would be a presentation on the Relationship between Dimensionality and Quantum Mechanics.

My fingertips began to tingle as vicarious stage fright triggered my adrenal glands.

"Is this speech any good?" Brenda whispered.

I shook my head. "No idea."

A man I didn't recognize walked onto the stage and smiled at the audience. "It is my very great pleasure," he said, "to introduce one of our nation's leading voices in scientific thought, philosophy, and sociology. Our guest this morning has more advanced degrees than I have time to read, so let me get out of the way and allow our speaker to take the stage. Ladies and gentlemen, I give you Dr. James McKinney."

Polite applause filled the auditorium as the professor stepped onto the stage and blinked in the bright lights. Instead of proceeding immediately to the lectern as he usually did, he walked to a stool in the middle of the stage and took a seat.

"In a few months I will be sixty-one years old," he said, not even glancing at the typed pages in his hand, "and as a man enters the final seasons of his life, he has a tendency to look over the road he has traveled and question his choices—the job not taken, the pregnancy terminated, the shift in careers. The woman left behind."

Though I kept my gaze on the professor, from the corner of my eye I saw Tank look at me, his brow lifted. He wanted to know what the professor meant, but I knew no more about the professor's unusual approach than Tank did.

"Imagine," the professor continued, "that you are holding a strip of paper only one atom high and several microns long." The professor set his notes on a lectern, then spread his hands as if indicating a long strip of paper. "You are holding an object that exists, for all practical purposes, in only two dimensions: height and length. Agreed?"

He looked out at the audience, and as one, we nodded.

The professor smiled. "Now take one end of your imaginary paper and join it to the other so it makes a circle. If you were a tiny sugar ant, you could travel on that paper—over its length—without ever leaving the second dimension. But if you twisted the paper, so that the upper side joined the lower side at the junction point, a sugar ant could literally cross over to the underside of that paper and enter a world of three dimensions—height, length, and width, because you would be able to travel on the *front* and *back* of the one-atom width. Correct?"

We nodded again, but less collectively this time. I glanced at Tank, whose forehead had crinkled. Brenda was thinking hard, too, and even Daniel had looked up from his electronic game.

At least no one was bored.

"Einstein said time travel should be possible," the professor went on. "All we have to do is find a way to fold dimensions so we can move from one to the other. If we discover a way to do that, a man ought to be able to choose a point early in his life and revisit it, making new choices the second time."

The professor smiled as a murmur rippled through the crowd. "Ah, now I have your attention. Yes, time is the fourth dimension, and the fifth and sixth dimensions are planes of possibilities. If I left my current starting point and moved to the sixth dimension, I could find myself in an auditorium like this and face vastly different options. If I could fold over to the seventh dimension, I could find myself in a jungle or on a different planet, because the seventh dimension is composed of possibilities that merge not from my *current* starting point, but from the beginning of time. The eighth dimension includes the histories of all possible universes, and the ninth, all possible everythings. The tenth dimension is limitless, and includes every possible thing anyone could imagine."

The professor stood, his eyes wide with the infinite variety of alternatives he was imagining. I found myself caught up in his fervor, and I barely heard him as he went on to compare dimensionality with inflationary cosmology and our expanding universe, which theoretically creates room for more universes. I was familiar with the cosmology material because my friends and I had met people and creatures from other universes, but I still found the concept mind-boggling.

"Snogg . . . rmph." I elbowed Tank, who was contentedly snoring beside me.

I tried to follow the rest of the professor's presentation, but his idea of time travel through folded dimensions had opened a door, and I spent the rest of the hour imagining the possibilities.

Chapter 4

"Honestly, professor." I caught his arm as Tank, Brenda, and Daniel scooted past us into the house. "You did a great job. That may have been the best presentation I've ever heard on the subject of time travel and dimensionality."

I expected him to brush me off—after all, the professor has never been one to easily pocket praise. But he held my gaze and the corner of his mouth wobbled. "You really think so?"

"I wouldn't say it if I didn't mean it." I released his arm and jerked my thumb toward the narrow path that led to the beach. "Want to join us down on the beach? I think you deserve to relax a little now that your big speech is over."

"Maybe later." He smiled, then walked into the house and down the hall. I followed, on the way to my room, but lifted a brow when the professor went into his room and pointedly closed the door.

Okay, then. Maybe he needed some time to decompress.

I blew out a breath. I was hoping the professor would snap out of his preoccupation once he'd finished his presentation, but he seemed just as abstracted as he had when we left the house. Was something else bothering him? Something I hadn't even guessed?

"Hey, Andi!"

I turned at the sound of Tank's voice and found him in the living room . . . all wrapped up in a metal detector. Headphones covered his ears, a harness and elbow braced supported some kind of screen/joystick apparatus, and a circular disk on the end of a stick hovered above the carpeted floor.

I gave the contraption a skeptical look. "So that's it, huh? You're serious about this?"

He grinned. "I thought you might want a demonstration. Happy to show you the ropes."

"Maybe later." I forced a smile. "Let me change into shorts, then I"ll come outside."

"See you later, then." He went through the kitchen, then out the sliding glass doors and onto the deck. Maybe Daniel would enjoy helping him look for buried treasure or whatever. I wasn't particularly thrilled by the idea.

I was about to go back to my room, but the overabundance of light in the foyer reminded me that I'd left the door partly open. I stepped up to close it, and through the opening I glimpsed the two odd children I'd noticed yesterday. They were coming up the driveway, staring straight ahead, their arms hanging stiffly at their sides, neither of them smiling. Their deadpan expressions sent a cold hand down my spine—if they meant to creep me out, they were doing a good job of it.

But they were just *kids*, for heaven's sake.

Abby, who stood by my side looking out the sidelights, saw the kids and stiffened. Then she began to growl.

"Easy, Abs." I pasted on a bright smile and stepped onto the front porch, closing the door firmly behind me. "Can I help you with something?"

They halted in unison, then the boy swiveled his head and met my gaze. "Will you let us come in?" he asked, his voice flat and matter-of-fact.

I looked at the girl, who had also turned her head to look at me. "Is this some kind of joke? Maybe a dare?" I asked. I softened my smile. "Are you two lost or something?"

They didn't answer. The girl stared at me, and something in her unwavering gaze lifted the hair at the back of my neck. "Will you let us in?" she asked in the same dull tone as the boy. "It will only take a minute."

"*What* will only take a minute?"

"We need to use the telephone," the boy said, staring at me without even blinking.

I hesitated. Most kids in this neighborhood carried cell phones that served as invisible leashes connecting them to their parents. With all the tourist traffic on this street, I couldn't imagine any parent sending their kids out without one.

And something—some atavistic alarm signal—

warned me not to let these kids in the house.

"Um . . . I'll call someone for you, if you want to give me a number."

Nothing flickered in their eyes—not interest, not gratitude, not even curiosity. "Will you let us in?" the boy repeated. "It will only take a minute."

My heart hammered in my chest as I stepped back toward the door.

"Let us in," the girl echoed, stepping forward in lockstep with the boy. "It will only take a minute."

That's when I smelled it—a scent of death and dying things, an odor so repulsive that my gag reflex kicked in. I made an effort to look away, then took another step backward. When I felt the threshold beneath the sole of my shoe, I spun and moved inside, slamming the door behind me. I flipped the deadbolt, then leaned against the solid wood, relishing its strength beneath my clammy palms. Abby stood next to me, her nose pressed to the crack between the door and the doorframe, hair lifted along her spine.

Only when my heart had calmed did I move to the peephole and look outside.

No one stood on the porch. No kids walked down the driveway. Since our porch faced the side of the property, I could see the Diaz house, where a giant sabal palm rattled its leaves in the breeze.

I was about to turn away when I saw them again—the boy and girl were walking up the sidewalk that led to the Diaz's front door.

This was not good. I don't know how I knew it, but I knew that if I did nothing, I would feel like I had walked away from someone drowning . . .

"Andi! Aren't you coming?"

I turned, dry-mouthed, and saw Brenda and Daniel

standing behind me in bathing suits, beach towels slung over their shoulders. I could smell coconut-scented sunscreen from where I stood—a far cry from the nauseating odor I'd inhaled a few minutes before.

"I'll be right out," I said, rummaging in my purse for my cell phone. "I just have to make a quick call."

I dialed 911, then hesitated when the operator answered. How was I supposed to explain the panic I felt around those kids?

"I'm not sure this is an emergency," I finally told her, "but two kids are wandering down Gulf Boulevard and asking people to let them into their homes. They seem sort of—I don't know, maybe shell-shocked, and I'm afraid they may have been involved in something—"

"Ma'am? What are you saying?"

"I think they've been involved in something really bad. Maybe you could send someone to check on them?"

The woman took my name and address, then thanked me and promised to send a patrol car.

Feeling that I'd done my duty, I moved on down the hall, ready to put on my bathing suit and join the others. Before going to my room, though, I peeked into the other's bedrooms to make sure they had plenty of towels.

I paused in the room Brenda was using—her sketch book lay on her bed, open to a drawing that immediately caught my attention. On the page I saw the two children, and in the stark lines of a number two pencil I finally realized what had alarmed me most about those kids.

Their eyes. Their eyes were solid black—no white,

no iris, no color at all. Just solid orbs as dark as a starless night sky.

I caught Brenda down on the beach. "Your sketch," I said, dropping to the towel I'd spread on the sand. "Forgive me for snooping, but I couldn't help seeing your sketchbook on the bed. When did you draw those kids?"

She frowned. "The image came to me during the professor's presentation. But don't tell him I was sketching during his talk. I'll never hear the end of it."

"Wait—did you see them at the university?"

She looked at me as if I'd been out in the sun too long. "I didn't see them with my *eyes*. I just *saw* them, so I drew them." She snorted softly. "Why? You got spooky kids hidden in the attic or something?"

"They walked up to the house while you and Daniel were changing into your bathing suits."

Her arched brows lifted. "Shut. Up. You're kiddin', right?"

I shook my head. "I wish. Because they are every bit as creepy as they look in your picture. But I didn't realize why they creeped me out until I saw your sketch—it's those eyes. But not only their eyes— everything about them is somehow *off*. Their speech, their posture, their clothing—it's like they're from the back side of the moon."

Brenda's eyes narrowed. "Maybe they are."

"And they stink. I've never smelled a dead body, but something tells me it would smell just like those kids." I shifted my gaze to the surf, where Tank and Daniel were walking around with the metal detector and studying the sand. "Here we go again. I was really hoping we'd have some time to relax. The professor could certainly use some down time."

"Ditto," Brenda said. "I love takin' care of Daniel, but I tell ya—being a full-time parent is a lot harder than I thought. And Daniel's not exactly a regular kid."

"Is he giving you problems?"

"Nothing I can't work out. Trouble is, I'm so busy bouncing between work and taking care of him that my time, patience, and creativity are in short supply. So I was glad when you invited us to come for some beach time. Even if we have to deal with crazy stuff, it's good to be with you guys. I know you love Daniel, too, and that takes some of the pressure off."

I gave her a sympathetic smile and remained silent while she rolled onto her stomach and pillowed her head on her hands. The beach was quiet, probably because it was a weekday and as hot as blazes. Maybe the rest of the week would be quiet and peaceful. After all, we hadn't received any directions or plane tickets from the mysterious people who usually sent us on strange ventures. But Brenda had received a vision of those kids and I had actually met them, so the odds that we were about to be caught up in some bizarre situation were growing greater all the time—

"Andi!"

Uh oh. What now?

I turned at the sound of the professor's voice. He stood on the edge of the back deck, and when he caught my gaze, he pointed to the house. "Someone here to see you!"

Who knew I was home?

Grumbling under my breath, I stood, picked up my towel, and shook it carefully so it wouldn't spray sand all over Brenda. "Looks like I gotta go. You think we should grill hamburgers for dinner?"

"Whatever," Brenda murmured, her eyes closed. "Let me know when, and I'll help."

"Okay."

I wrapped my towel around my chest and started toward the house.

By the time I reached the house, I remembered that I'd given my address to the 911 dispatcher. I was expecting to find an officer or two in the living room, but instead I found Mr. Diaz distractedly petting Abby in the foyer. Perspiration dotted his forehead, his thinning hair was disheveled, and his eyes were wide with fear.

I regretted taking my time about coming up the hill. "Mr. Diaz." I tucked my towel more firmly under my arm and hurried toward him. "Is everything okay?"

His face suddenly rippled with anguish. "Have you seen Maria? I came home and the door was standing open. She's not in the house. I've been through it twice, looking everywhere, and she's not there."

"Maybe—" I spoke slowly in an effort to counter his increasing panic— "maybe she went to the store to pick up something for dinner."

"Her car's still in the driveway. Her purse is still on the counter where we drop things. Her keys are still in her purse."

I frowned. "Could she have gone down to the beach?"

"She hates the beach, especially now that she's pregnant. She says she can't see her feet anymore, let alone get sand off them."

He was pacing now, moving toward the front door, then striding back to me. "I hoped she'd come over here to borrow something, or to talk to your grandmother—"

"Sabba and Safta are in New York for the week."

"So have you seen Maria at all?"

"Not today." I patted his arm. "I saw her yesterday, and she was fine. But we were at the university this morning and got back about an hour ago."

"Did you see anything? Any strangers? A prowler? A salesman?"

I wanted to say no, but I *had* seen someone—the black-eyed children. And every instinct in my body had warned me against them.

"I did see two kids I didn't recognize. And about twenty minutes ago they were walking toward your house."

"Kids? Like from the neighborhood?"

I bit my lip. "I don't think so. They were . . . odd. They came to our door and asked if they could come inside."

Mr. Diaz blinked. "Why? What did they want?"

"They said they wanted to use the phone, but something about them put me off so much that I called the police when they left. I watched them cross our driveway and head for your house."

Mr. Diaz went pale, and might have collapsed if the professor hadn't stepped out of the dining room and slid a chair beneath the panicked husband. "I know my wife," Mr. Diaz said, his voice trembling. "If two kids asked her for help, she'd give them whatever they wanted."

"They didn't exactly ask for help," I clarified. "They asked if they could use the telephone."

Diaz blinked several times. "Why didn't you let them?"

I shifted my weight beneath a load of unexpected guilt. "It . . . felt wrong to let them in. And Abby was growling, so I didn't think it'd be a good idea."

"Were they some kind of gypsies? Do you think they were part of a gang? Could they be runners for some kind of drug cartel—"

"Relax, man, I'm sure your wife is fine," the professor said.

I shot him a grateful smile, glad that he'd stepped out to help.

"This isn't like Maria." Mr. Diaz shook his head. "I'm worried sick. The baby could come at any time. What if she's hurt or something?"

Whirling blue lights appeared in the window, so I gestured to the vehicle outside. "The police have arrived. Why don't we go see if they have any news?"

Chapter 5

Brenda, Daniel, Tank, the professor, and I stood at the window and watched as two police officers questioned Mr. Diaz. The poor man was nearly in tears, his hands flying in frustrated gestures, his face taut with fear and worry.

"They always suspect the spouse," Brenda said, eying Mr. Diaz with a narrowed gaze. "Seems like nine times out of ten, the husband did it."

"We don't know for sure if anybody did anything," I pointed out. "And I was talking to Mrs. Diaz just yesterday, while Mr. Diaz was at work. She seemed very happy and was excited about the coming baby."

The professor said nothing, but slowly ran his

fingers over his silver beard.

"Dear Lord." For a moment I thought Tank was using a figure of speech, then I realized he was praying. "Lord," he continued, not bothering to close his eyes, "please lead the police to Mrs. Diaz, and keep her safe. Place your angels around her—"

"Anoił," Daniel interrupted.

"—and keep her safe from the evil one."

"Duch," Daniel said.

"Daniel," I asked, following a sudden whim, "look around outside. Do you see . . . anyone or anything we should know about?"

Though Daniel can sometimes adopt autistic behaviors when it comes to interaction with others, he seemed to understand what I meant. He moved closer to the window, pressed his hands to the glass, and peered out at the Diaz house, even tilting his head to look upward in case any unseen entities hovered nearby.

Finally he shook his head and Brenda drew him closer in a protective embrace. "Good to know," she said simply. "You neighbor probably went out for coffee."

"Would you go out for coffee and leave your purse behind?" I asked.

Brenda shrugged. "Sure would. If my friend was paying."

I wanted to believe her, but a dark foreboding had settled into my gut and refused to go away. One by one, the others left the window—the professor went back to his room, Brenda and Daniel went into the kitchen, and Tank curled up for a nap on the sofa with Abby.

But I couldn't rest while Mrs. Diaz was missing. I

went outside and sat on the steps of the front porch, watching quietly as the police went into my neighbor's house with Mr. Diaz. When they came out a few minutes later, I overhead their parting remarks. "We can't file an official missing persons report until a party has been missing twenty-four hours," the older officer said. "But given her condition and your neighbor's observation of those kids, we'll issue a bulletin to the officers on patrol. If they see her, they'll radio in."

Mr. Diaz thanked them, then waited on the porch, his hands in his pockets, while the officers drove away.

Before he went into the house, Mr. Diaz lifted his head and caught my gaze. His eyes, so filled with despair and anxiety, sent a wave of melancholy rushing over me, and in that moment I wished I felt free to pray aloud like Tank often did. He summoned supernatural help in a voice that reassured and comforted, whereas my prayer would sound more like a whimper.

Mr. Diaz turned and went into his house, and from where I sat I heard the click of his deadbolt.

But I didn't think a deadbolt could thwart the sort of evil we were about to encounter.

After dinner, Brenda came over and dropped her sketchbook into my lap. "No idea what this means," she said, folding her arms. "But I saw it clear as day, which means it's probably gonna happen."

I picked up the paper and stared at an image of myself. I was standing in the center of what looked like a crop circle, and I was staring up at the sky as I held a bundle in my arms. My eyes were wide and my lips parted—as if I'd just seen something that scared me spitless.

"Any idea where that could be?" Brenda asked.

I shook my head. "This is the coast—no one grows crops around here."

"Then I guess you'd better get ready to take a trip."

I glanced across the room, where Tank was watching with concern in his eyes. "Are you gonna be in danger, Andi?"

"I don't see how." I shrugged. "Maybe we're all just a little confused."

"Yeah, right." Brenda snorted, then went back to the jigsaw puzzle she and Daniel were working on. I tried to pick up my book and resume reading, but the image of that sketch keep floating across the back of my eyelids.

Chapter 6

A shrill ringing blasted me from bed at seven a.m. I reached for the house phone on a tide of dread, afraid something had happened to one of my grandparents, but Mr. Diaz was on the line, his words coming at double-speed. "They found Maria. She's at the hospital, though they won't tell me anything else. Can you come? The police will be there, and they want to ask more questions about *los ninos*."

"They want to ask *me* questions?" I shook my head to clear away the fog of sleep. "About those kids?"

"*Por favor*, Andi, *¿puede venir?*"

"I'll come," I promised. "As soon as I get dressed, I'll meet you at the hospital. Oh—and I'm glad they found your wife."

I hung up before fully considering the implication of Mr. Diaz's words—his wife was in the *hospital* and the police had questions to ask. So Maria Diaz had definitely not slipped out for coffee with a friend.

Maybe I should have slipped away quietly, but by the time I'd dressed and left my room, Tank, Brenda and Daniel, and the professor were munching on cereal and toaster pastries at the breakfast table. I explained that I was going to the hospital to see Mrs. Diaz, and, either out of curiosity or *esprit de corp*s, everyone else decided to come along.

When we arrived at Suncoast Hospital, we found Mr. Diaz in the waiting room outside the elevator. To my surprise, he appeared nearly as upset as he had been yesterday.

"Your wife," I said, grasping his clenched hand when he stood to greet us. "She's okay, right?"

His eyes filled with tears. "She is fine. But the baby—our baby is missing."

I blinked. "What?"

Words spilled from his mouth. "The police are in there now with the doctor. The baby is gone, but the doctors say Maria did not give birth. There are no marks of surgery, no tearing, no evidence the baby was born. The doctors say the—what is the word?— placenta? It is still in place. They will have to go in and remove it or Maria could get sick."

"That's impossible," Brenda said, her voice flat. "The baby floats inside the placenta. If the baby's been born, the placenta should be gone, too."

"That's what the doctors say." Mr. Diaz's wide eyes met Brenda's. "But the baby is gone! It has been stolen from her—"

"Wait a minute, let's remain in the realm of actual realities." The professor put a steadying arm on Mr. Diaz's shoulder. "Where was your wife found?"

"In a field, just off the main road, lying in the grass like some cast off garbage." Mr. Diaz sank into a chair as his voice trembled. "An officer called for an ambulance, and they brought her here, to the hospital. The doctors examined her and right away, they said they could not hear a heartbeat. And then they discovered that the baby was gone. But they do not know who took it, or even how they took it and she will not awaken to tell us anything—"

He buried his face in his hands, silently shutting us out. I looked at the others, who appeared as confused and bewildered as I felt.

"She's not waking up?" The professor arched a brow. "She must have been drugged."

"With what?" I asked. "If she has, surely something would show up in a blood test."

The professor glanced at his watch. "They haven't had time to run a tox screen. Maybe we'll get an answer to that question later."

"We're missing something obvious here," Brenda insisted. "Babies don't just disappear from the womb. Someone's missing evidence that ought to be clearly visible—"

I held my finger across my lips, then gestured to Mr. Diaz, who didn't need to hear our wild speculations. "Let's go to the cafeteria and talk. I can do some Internet searches to see if anything like this has ever happened before. But before we go, I need to know something."

I knelt in front of Mr. Diaz and squeezed his arm. "Mr. Diaz, did the police tell you anything about those strange kids?"

Mr. Diaz blinked as if my question didn't register, then he shook his head. With his baby missing and his wife unresponsive, those kids were the farthest thing from his mind.

I released his arm and stood, then followed the others to the elevator.

Because the cafeteria was crowded, we gathered in a small group of chairs near the snack machines. Brenda fished quarters out of her purse to buy Daniel a carton of juice while I sank into a chair and pulled out my phone to do some Googling. Tank sat next to me, his hands in his pockets, looking uncomfortable and completely out of his element. I think he'd been ready to bolt ever since Brenda uttered the word *placenta*.

"Pregnant woman's baby disappears," I murmured as I typed the phrase into the search engine. I pressed the search key, then caught my breath. "Yikes! Several links here."

"I'll bet most of them are associated with conspiracy websites," Brenda said, sitting across from me. "Seems like I saw something like that in a movie—or am I thinking of the monster who laid its eggs inside the woman's belly?"

I clicked on a link and skimmed the article. "This report is purely scientific. According to this, a woman pregnant with twins might find that one of the twins has been absorbed into the other. Apparently that's rare, but it happens."

"But your neighbor wasn't carrying twins," Tank pointed out. "And she was huge."

"She *was* pretty far along in her pregnancy," I said, amending his statement because no woman, not even a pregnant one, wants to be called *huge*. "And yeah, Brenda, you're right—I see several pages about unborn babies being stolen by aliens."

"Told you," Brenda said. "Kooks rule the Internet."

"But we've seen unbelievable things, and we're not kooks," I reminded her. "I mean, we've seen houses that disappear and reappear, happy nuns that escort us from one universe to another, monsters in fog, killer slime—"

"Daniel and I came here for a *vacation*," Brenda said, practically glaring at me. "This wasn't supposed to be another romp in the twilight zone."

Tank grinned at her. "Can we help it if the Twilight Zone keeps drawing us in?" He nudged me with his elbow. "What about those alien reports? Anything that sounds like your neighbor's story?"

I skimmed several posts on an electronic bulletin board. "Okay, here's a guy who says a woman he knows lost her baby when aliens abducted her. She was found the next day, but she wasn't pregnant any more. And doctors couldn't tell how the baby was removed."

"Bingo," Tank said.

I was about to argue, but my mouth went dry when someone down the hall released a blood-curdling scream.

Brenda stared toward the sound. "Isn't that near—"

Drawn by the horrific wail, we stood and walked toward the commotion, which proved to be coming from Maria Diaz's room. A couple of cops waited outside the open door, and they looked as helpless as I felt. I peered around the doorframe and saw that Maria had regained consciousness, but she was flailing and screaming, her eyes wide with terror. "No, no!" she screamed. "*¡No me toques! ¡No vienen cerca de mí !*"

The nurse was trying to wrap Maria's arms in restraints, but she was no match for the panicked woman. The doctor kept barking the name of some drug, but the nurse had her hands full with the restraints—

Another nurse and an orderly ran past us and attempted to help. But while a nurse injected a drug into the IV line, Maria's gaze fell on her husband and her chin trembled. "*Tomaron nuestro bebé*," she said, her voice breaking. "They said they were going to take the baby."

"*¿Quien?*" Mr. Diaz stroked his wife's hair. "Honey, who are you talking about?"

"*Los monstruos*," she said, her eyelids drooping as the drug took effect. "*Los grises*. The ones . . . the *chicos* . . . *esos chicos me llevaron a ellos*." Her eyes closed and she stopped speaking.

Mr. Diaz looked at the doctor, who shook his head. "She's obviously not herself," the doctor said. "Probably hallucinating. Does your wife use any sort of recreational drugs?"

"No!" Mr. Diaz recoiled from the question. "She never has, and she never would, not with the baby! She'd never do anything to hurt our child."

Mr. Diaz stepped away from the doctor, and his gaze crossed mine as he looked toward the door. Then he set his jaw and strode toward us, meeting me and the others out in the hallway.

"Where's that detective?" he asked, looking

around. "She said those kids—" he swallowed hard—
"took her to monsters who took our baby. I want to
know who they are, and I want them found. I don't
know what they're up to, but I want them found and
arrested."

As he stalked off in search of the police, I turned
to the others. "*Los grises*," I repeated. "Anybody know
what that means?"

Tank shrugged, then we all looked at the
professor, who cleared his throat before answering:
"The gray ones."

Brenda, Daniel, Tank, and I went back to the
house, leaving the professor with Mr. Diaz. For some
reason my neighbor seemed to take comfort from the
professor's calm demeanor, and for the first time I
began to see why James McKinney might have been
an effective priest in his former profession. When he
wasn't arguing, he could be a compassionate listener,
and that's what he was doing with Mr. Diaz—
listening.

When the professor finally arrived back at the
house, he sat in the living room and we gathered
around him. "Typical abduction story," he said,
glancing up at me as he propped his feet on the
ottoman. "Could have been scripted from *The X-Files*.
Woman is home, kids knock on the door, she lets
them in. Next thing she knows, she wakes up in the
hospital bed and she's not pregnant any more."

"What about the things she was saying?" I asked.
"Talking about the gray ones and telling them to stay
away from her."

The professor shrugged. "If those are actual

memories, they're buried somewhere in her subconscious. She may recall them in dreams or while under the influence of drugs or hypnosis, but I was there when the police questioned her, and she couldn't remember anything."

"They still got her tied down?" Brenda's eyes narrowed. "I hate it when doctors wrap people up like dangerous animals."

"She's calm now, so they removed the restraints. She'll be able to come home tomorrow if there are no complications."

"But what about the baby?" I asked. "She was really pregnant, nearly full term. You can't tell me *that* baby somehow got reabsorbed into her body."

"The attending physician thought it might be a hysterical pregnancy," the professor said, "until Mrs. Diaz's obstetrician arrived. She opened her laptop and pulled up ultrasounds that showed a normal, healthy baby in the womb."

"What about those strange kids?" I asked. "Have the police found *them*? What did Maria remember about them?"

The professor's mouth quirked. "Not much, and no, the police haven't found them. No one else has even seen them." He glanced around. "Is anyone else ready for dinner? I'm starving. I didn't lower myself to raiding the snack machines like you guys did."

I went off to dig through Sabba's collection of take out menus, but I couldn't get Mrs. Diaz and those kids out of my mind.

After dinner, the conversation turned to weird kids. I tried to do an Internet search, but the terms "strange kids" and "odd children" didn't bring up anything other than stories about parents contemplating the difficulty of child-rearing.

But then I remembered the oddest thing about those kids, the thing Brenda caught in her sketch: the black eyes. And my first search for "black-eyed kids" brought up exactly what I was searching for.

"Listen to this entry about black-eyed children," I said, interrupting Tank's story about a toddler who could throw a football for fifty yards. "According to an urban legend, unusual children with completely black eyes have been spotted in various neighborhoods around the world. These children— called BEKs—reportedly knock on strangers' doors, usually at night, and ask to be let in. Most people report feeling an unusual sense of dread or fear in the presence of these children, and evil is supposed to befall the hapless person who falls for their disguise and let them in."

"*Disguise*?" Brenda interrupted. "If they're not kids, what are they?"

I held up a finger and kept reading. "Explanations of these and other strange appearances go back through the ages. In China and Japan, folklore reveals stories of vengeful ghosts, hungry apparitions that appear and demand to be fed. Those who do not submit to the ghosts' demands meet with bad luck or illness. Europe compares them to vampires, tales from the Middle East offer stories of the Djinn, supernaturally empowered beings from which we get the word *genie*. Some say the BEKs are manifestations of dark thoughts; in the middle ages, they might have been considered changelings, soulless children substituted for real children by the fairies. Stories of these black-eyed children, who seem poorly adapted to contemporary social situations and skills, have been around since the 1990s."

"Urban legend, huh?" Tank smiled a humorless smile. "That means the story's not true, right?"

"Sometimes," I answered, "but sometimes not. Sometimes people label stories as urban legends just because there doesn't appear to be a logical explanation for the story's events. But sometimes the answers to those stories lies beyond our current understanding."

"Some people," the professor inserted, "believe that aliens seek human babies in order to create hybrids that are half-human, half-alien. Others say that the culprits are human beings—government types who are using alien DNA to create hybrids for military purposes."

"Sounds like something the Gate would be interested in," I said. "Human-alien hybrids to colonize another planet—"

"Or live under the sea," the professor added. "Who knows what they're planning?"

"That makes no sense," Brenda said. "Why would anyone want to mix our races?"

"Our *species*," I corrected. "Our races are already mixed—people on this planet have become so mingled that we're all human mutts. If you're talking about mingling humans and aliens, you'd be talking about two different species."

"Still." She shook her head. "If aliens are so superior, why don't they just wipe us out and take over the planet? That's what they want in all those science fiction movies."

"Hang on a minute." Tank's eyes had taken on a

deeply thoughtful look. "I know I usually don't add much to these conversations, but bear with me, okay? I don't believe in aliens—not from outer space, anyway. I mean, if alien beings lived on Mars or even the moon, don't you think we would have seen some evidence of their existence? We've sent cameras up there. We've filled the galaxy with space junk—if there were other civilized species in space, don't you think we would have seen some of *their* space junk floating around? Something? We've sent cameras pretty doggone far into space, and they haven't been able to prove that anything's out there."

"A lot of people have seen UFOs," Brenda pointed out. "And a lot of other people claim to have been abducted by aliens. They can't all be crazy."

"I don't think they're crazy," Tank said. "I think maybe these creatures, whatever they are, aren't from other planets. Maybe they're coming from other dimensions, or other worlds—like Helga or the monsters in the fog. We know the other worlds exist, and we know they can come through certain portals. So maybe these other things are plenty real, they're just not what we think they are."

Brenda crossed her arms. "That still doesn't answer the question about why they'd want a hybrid species."

Tank shifted his weight and sighed heavily. "I thought of something," he said slowly, "but I'm not sure I want to tell you. Might be like casting pearls before swine."

Brenda stiffened. "Are you calling us *pigs*?"

Tank's face went the color of a tomato. "No, no— it's just an expression. But I've got an uncle who's a preacher, and he says that the devil has always been trying to thwart God's plan to redeem the human race. So back in the old days, he sent demons to make babies with human women—it's in the Bible. Those babies grew up to be giants, and they were around even after Noah's flood. Some of them had six fingers and six toes, so I guess you could say they were hybrids."

I blinked. Being Jewish, I'd heard Torah stories all my life, but I'd never heard anything about demonic hybrids. "Where in the Bible?" I asked, staring hard at Tank. "That sounds crazy."

"Genesis," Tank answered. "The story of the Nephilim."

"That story," the professor said in a soothing voice, "has been interpreted in various ways. Some say those who fathered the giants were merely exalted men, not spiritual beings like angels or demons. I would cast my vote in that direction."

Tank shrugged, leaving the professor with the last word, but I wasn't convinced the professor was right. Since leaving the priesthood, he had a tendency to automatically reject any explanation that had to do with God, but his explanation of the Nephilim did not explain how "exalted men" could create a race of giants.

"Maybe we don't have to know all the answers—at least not yet," I said. "Seems to me the most important thing is helping Mrs. Diaz find her baby."

"If the kid has been whisked into another dimension," Brenda said, frowning, "good luck with that."

Chapter 7

Later that night I sat at the desk in the study, searching the Internet for stories of fetal abductions. Rain had been falling since before sunrise, so none of us were in the mood to go outside and sunbathing was out of the question. I kept looking out the window at the Diaz house, hoping to see Mr. Diaz bringing his wife home, but apparently they were still at the hospital.

I looked up when I heard a soft cough from the hallway. The professor was standing in the doorway, looking at me with a strange look on his face.

"Andi," he said, his face blanketed by a peaceful expression I rarely saw him wear, "if I take a picture on my phone, can you print it for me?"

"Sure." I gestured toward the machine in the corner. "That printer does a pretty good job with photos. How big do you want it?"

"Small. Pocket-size." He flashed a smile, then tilted his head toward the den. "Join me in the other room, will you?"

Curious, I followed him to the family room, where Daniel was playing a video game, Brenda was sitting on the carpeted floor and looking at magazines, and Tank was snoring on the sofa. The professor stood in the center of the room and cleared his throat. When Tank didn't stop snoring, Brenda punched his shoe.

"If I may have your attention," the professor said, casting his gaze around the room, "I'd like to commemorate this occasion with a group photo. You'll all have to gather around and squeeze in tightly for this selfie to work."

Brenda frowned. "You want a picture now? I don't have my eyelashes on."

"Just something to remember this little trip," the professor answered. "I'm not expecting white tie and full makeup."

Tank threw me a questioning look, and so did Brenda. I shrugged, not having the faintest clue what the professor was up to. He wasn't sentimental, and this trip wasn't exactly worth commemorating, in my view. But if he wanted to do something to remember this trip, why not humor him?

"Come on," I said, stepping to the professor's side. "You too, Daniel. You're gonna have to leave your game for a minute."

Feeling awkward and clumsy, we all gathered around the professor and smiled at the phone in his hand. He, of course, didn't smile, but carefully adjusted the phone until we were all visible on the screen, then he pressed the button. The phone responded by playing the sound of a shutter click, then the professor nodded. "Resume whatever you were doing," he said, stepping out of the huddle. "Andi, can you print this image for me?"

I led the way back to my grandfather's study. "What's this about?" I asked, glancing at the professor. "Are you doing some kind of experiment, or getting sentimental in your old age?"

"Neither." He gave me a tight-lipped smile and pressed keys on his phone. "I've just sent the image to your email account, so if you could print it . . ."

"Pocket-sized?"

"Correct. Just slip it beneath my door after you've trimmed it. Thank you."

He turned toward his room, but before leaving he caught my shoulder, stepped closer, and planted a kiss on my forehead. "Dear Andi," he whispered, his voice growing rough. "You are the daughter I might have had . . . if I'd made different choices along the way."

I blinked, my thoughts stuttering in surprise, while he released me and returned to his room, closing the door behind him.

Chapter 8

The next morning I rose early and made waffles—my grandmother's recipe, complete with the secret ingredient of almond extract, which filled the kitchen with a scrumptious aroma. I wanted the team to be in a good mood because I hoped to enlist them in my search for Mrs. Diaz's missing baby.

The scents of waffles and sizzling bacon did the trick. Tank came into the kitchen right after I'd finished cooking, and Daniel and Brenda followed soon after. Brenda went outside and brought in the newspaper, then we all sat down to eat. The professor's seat, however, remained empty, and I kept glancing at it, wondering if he was working or had decided to sleep late.

"Look at these shoes," Brenda said, holding up the front of the Lifestyles section. "Ten inch platforms. I'd need a ladder to climb into those things."

"I don't think they're meant to be walked in." I shrugged. "Aren't those things just for fashion shows?"

"The Reds traded for a new first baseman," Tank announced, as if anybody at the table cared. "They have several good players on their farm teams. Wonder why they didn't just move them up?"

I blew out a breath, not knowing how to respond to Tank because I knew next to nothing about baseball. I looked at Daniel, who had put down his handheld video game and allowed his gaze to drift over the abandoned local news section on the table. Then he put his finger on the paper and slid it over, across the table, until it rested in front of me. "Read," he said, not meeting my gaze.

I picked up the paper and scanned the largest headline: Local Youth Contracts Mysterious Illness. My pulse skittered.

With increasing alarm, I read the story. According to the newspaper article, Georgia Hanson had run into a mini market while her son Jax waited in the family van. When she returned, another child was sitting in the van with her son. Alarmed, she opened the back door to see who the child was. She asked for his name, but he kept his head down and didn't answer. Instead Jax said, "He wanted to come in, so I let him."

Alarmed, Mrs. Hanson ordered the unknown boy out of the car. He obeyed, not speaking, but when he left the car, he looked directly at her, and that's when she panicked—the boy appeared unusually pale and wan. She instinctively glanced at her son, who was still sitting in the back seat, and when she shifted to look again at the strange boy, he had vanished.

Almost immediately, Jax doubled over in pain, then passed out. Mrs. Hanson drove him to the emergency room, where the doctors examined him and could find nothing wrong. But Jax remained unconscious, and would remain in the hospital until he came out of his coma.

"Guys, listen to this." With a quaver in my voice, I read the news story to Brenda, Daniel, and Tank, pausing only long enough to look at the professor's empty seat and wish he'd hurry out to join us. I could sense a pattern in the odd events apparently precipitated by the black-eyed children, but I was too close to the story to see it. What did it all mean?

"Daniel," I said, lowering the newspaper, "would you go knock on the professor's door? Tell him we need him."

Daniel tilted his head and gave me a strange little smile. "He's gone."

"Gone?" Brenda blinked. "Gone where?"

Daniel held up his hand, pointed upward, and then rotated his hand as if he were pointing in all directions.

"This isn't a good time for guessing games," Brenda said, an edge to her voice. "If this is a joke, Daniel—"

I sincerely hoped it was. I left the table and walked down the hallway that led to the bedrooms, trying my best to ignore the ominous feeling in my gut.

I knocked on the professor's door and heard no

answer. Gathering my courage, I turned the doorknob . . . and realized that Daniel was right. The professor *was* gone, but he couldn't have gone far because his briefcase, his glasses, his laptop, and his current notebooks were still on the desk. But what I couldn't find, even when I searched the desktop and opened the lid of his suitcase, was the small photograph I had printed for him last night.

Abby, who had followed me into the room, sniffed the floor around the desk, then sniffed the professor's pajamas. Then she sat politely and tilted her head as if asking, "Well? Where'd he go?"

"I wish I knew, Abs."

Brenda came into the room as I was opening the professor's laptop. "Do you think he went out for coffee or something?"

I shook my head. "I was up early this morning, so I would have heard the alarm beep if anyone opened a door."

"Have you tried calling his cell phone?"

"Yeah. And I found his phone right over there, on the nightstand."

Brenda leaned against the doorframe. "Have you searched the house? Maybe he wanted a quiet place to think . . . or maybe he wanted to walk along the beach."

I gave her a *you've got to be kidding* look. "Have you ever known him to willingly walk on the beach?"

"Well . . . there's a first time for everything, right?"

"Yeah . . . but something tells me that this is a far bigger first time than we realize." I sank to the edge of the bed, where the blankets and pillow were neat and unrumpled. "Didn't his behavior yesterday strike you as odd?"

Brenda smirked. "The professor's always odd."

"But he's never asked for a group picture before. And there's more—last night, before he went into his room he kissed my forehead. It was . . . almost like he was saying goodbye."

Brenda's brow creased, then she shrugged. "I'll admit that he's seemed really preoccupied the last couple of days. But he'd be lost without you, Andi, so I hardly think he'd take off without telling you where he was going. And where would he go? Unless—" Her frown deepened. "You . . . you don't think he was thinkin' of offin' himself, do you?"

"No—no, definitely not. He wouldn't want a printed photo of our group if he was suicidal. He kept saying he wanted a pocket-sized copy of that image—"

"Maybe he wanted the cops to know who to contact . . . in case his body was mangled in a car crash or something."

"A list of names and phone number would be more helpful than a photo. Still, something's not right. I'm going to call the police."

Brenda sighed, then turned toward the hallway. "Honestly? The man's too stubborn to kill himself. But if you call the police, you're gonna feel really stupid when he comes in and yells at you for involving the cops."

"That's okay." I stood and moved toward the phone on the desk. "If I'm wrong, he can be as mad as he wants to be."

The police showed up within an hour of my call. Because I'd heard the cops tell Mr. Diaz that they couldn't file a missing persons report until twenty-four hours had passed, I was careful not to say that we wanted to report a missing person. Instead I told them that we'd awakened this morning and suspected that something had happened to the professor—foul play, perhaps. So could they please investigate, especially since something had also happened to the woman who lived next door . . .

My thoughts kept returning to the creepy kids. What if they had managed to get into the house? What if they'd met the professor?

The young cop leading the investigation—Officer Chad Edwards—suddenly stopped writing on his notepad and looked at me. "Haven't I seen you before?"

I felt an unwelcome blush creep onto my cheeks. "At the hospital, I think. I was there to see Mrs. Diaz. I saw you in the hallway."

"Yours is an easy face to remember." He smiled. "And what is your relationship to Dr. McKinney?"

"I'm his assistant. And before you ask, our relationship is strictly professional."

"Good to know." His smile deepened as he made a note on his pad.

From the sofa, Tank glowered at the cop. "Don't you want to dust for fingerprints or something? If someone broke in and kidnapped him—"

"No sign of forced entry," Edwards said. "And there's nothing missing or out of place, so an abduction is unlikely."

"Maybe," Brenda said. "But we're only guests here, so how would we know if something was missing?"

Officer Edwards ignored Brenda and smiled at me again. "Why don't you show me around and point out anything that seems odd to you?"

Brenda sighed dramatically and Tank stood, pulling himself upright and thrusting his sizable chest forward. I'd studied enough zoology to recognize male dominance behavior when I saw it, so more than anything I wanted Tank to calm down and behave himself. But if the professor was with those black-eyed kids, he might be sick or dying or in serious trouble . . .

I led the way to the bedroom the professor had been using. Everything was just as I'd left it—the laptop and notebooks on the table, his watch and phone on the nightstand, his pajamas still folded on the bed.

The cop's gaze fell on the pajamas. "Do you think he slept here last night?"

"Doesn't look like it."

"So maybe he went out. Could he have gone to a bar, someplace that stays open late?"

"No. I set the alarm when I went to bed, and I went to bed right after the professor went into his room. Dr. McKinney didn't know how to disarm the system. If he had opened a door or a window, the alarm would have gone off."

"Anyone else know how to disarm the security system?"

"My grandparents, but they're in New York. So I'm sure the professor didn't go out last night or this morning."

Edwards flipped his notebook closed and narrowed his eyes as he looked around. "If everything you say is true, then your missing professor vanished into thin air. We're missing something . . . because nobody ever vanishes without a trace."

I bit my lip, restraining the impulse to tell him about some of the things we had experienced as a group. "Sometimes they do," I whispered.

My cell phone rang just after I escorted the two policemen to the front door. My heart leapt in anticipation—maybe it was the professor—but caller ID identified the caller as Reuben Diaz, my neighbor.

"Andi," he said, after I greeted him, "I thought you should know that someone else has run into one of those black-eyed kids. There's a family at the hospital now; their little boy is upstairs in a coma. The wife saw a strange kid in her van and—"

"I read the story in the paper," I told him.

"Not all the story," Mr. Diaz said. "They didn't report everything. I talked to the mother myself. The kid in her van had black eyes."

I turned to face the others, who had gathered in the living room. Brenda, Tank, and Daniel were all looking at me, doubtless alarmed by the expression on my face.

"We're coming," I told him. "We'll meet you outside your wife's room."

After talking to Reuben Diaz, we found the Hanson family in the pediatric wing on the third floor. Jay Hanson lay in a hospital bed, his face still and pale as a heart monitor beeped and an IV line kept him hydrated.

Mrs. Hanson sat in a chair behind her son's bed, and Mr. Hanson was pacing in the narrow space between the end of the bed and the wall. A TV hung from the ceiling, but it was dark. Apparently no one felt like watching television.

"Mr. and Mrs. Hanson?" I asked, timidly stepping into the room. "My name is Andi Goldstein, and these are my friends Brenda, Tank, and Daniel."

The Hansons looked at us without reaction, but their gazes lingered on Daniel. "Is he—does he know Jax?" Mrs. Hanson asked. "Is he in Jax's class at school?"

I shook my head. "Daniel lives in California. We are here because . . . well, because the other day I had an encounter with two children with solid black eyes. I wondered if maybe we had . . . something in common."

Mrs. Hanson gasped and gripped the sheets on her son's bed. Her husband looked from her to me, then his face went a shade paler. "I wasn't sure . . . her story seemed so far-fetched."

"It's true," I said, meeting his gaze. "I've seen those kids twice, and there's something sinister about them. I can't explain it and I can understand why other people don't believe it—"

"The reporter didn't believe me," Mrs. Hanson said, her chin quivering. "I told her about that boy's eyes and she looked at me like I was crazy. She wrote down what I said, but she didn't put it in the paper. What good is a newspaper unless reporters are willing to tell the whole truth?"

I didn't have an answer to that, so I tried to change the subject. "Did the strange kid speak to you at all?"

"Not a word," she said. "He got out of the car when I told him to, though. Then he just disappeared. I glanced away only for a second, and he just vanished. I haven't stopped shaking since."

As if to prove her point, she lifted her hand so we could all see the tremor that quavered her fingertips.

"Has there been any change in your son?" Brenda asked, taking a step closer to the bed. She reached for Daniel's hand and held it tight as she looked down on the unconscious boy.

"None," Mr. Hanson answered. "He just lies there, and the doctors don't know why he won't wake up. They've done all kinds of scans and blood tests, but it's like something's got ahold of him and won't let go—"

Without saying a word, Tank stepped between me and Brenda, his gaze fixed on the boy's face. "Would you mind," he asked, not looking at either of the boy's parents, "if I prayed for your son?"

Mr. Hanson looked at his wife, but Mrs. Hanson kept her gaze focused on Tank. "I wish you would," she said, her voice heavy with unshed tears. "I don't know how to pray . . . for something like this."

I stepped back so Tank could move closer to the head of the bed, then we all watched as he placed his palm on the boy's forehead. "Lord," he prayed, "we know you are sovereign over all creation, over angels and demons, over all kinds of forces everywhere. We ask that you return this boy to his folks, binding whatever forces are keepin' him from wakin' up. Bring him back, Father, and wash his mind so that he don't have any memories of anything bad or evil. I ask these things humbly, but in the mighty name of Jesus, who holds authority over everything on and above and under the earth."

Silence fell over the room. Tank remained motionless, his hand on the boy's forehead, and no one spoke. Tears glistened on Mrs. Hanson's cheeks, and Mr. Hanson stared at his son as though he could bring his son back by the sheer force of his will. Brenda had bowed her head, too, though she might have been trying to hide her skepticism.

Daniel, on the other hand, was looking at the ceiling, his gaze traveling the width and breadth of the room as if he were watching creatures from other dimensions, forces who might be trying to steal this boy's soul . . . or return it.

I lowered my eyes as someone took a sharp breath. Jax Hanson's eyelids fluttered and color returned to his cheeks. His lower lip trembled, then his tongue darted over his lips and his eyes opened. "Mama? Dad?"

Tank lifted his hand and stepped back as a flush reddened his face and neck.

"Jax?" Mrs. Hanson rose and hovered over her son, her hands feeling his forehead, his cheeks. "Are you okay?"

"Where—what am I doing here?"

Jax attempted to sit up, but his father, who had rushed to his wife's side, held him back with a restraining hand. "Easy, son, you don't want to rush it."

"I feel fine. What's going on?"

Pssst.

I turned to see Tank in the doorway, already slinking away. Brenda stood behind him with Daniel, and they were waiting for me.

Leaving the Hansons alone with their son, I followed my friends down the hallway. "Wow," I said, completely at a loss for words. "Tank, what you did—"

"I didn't do anything," he said, gesturing toward

the elevators. "Come on, we should get going."

"If you didn't do it," Brenda countered, "then how in the heck did that kid get better?"

Tank didn't answer, but smiled as he pressed the elevator call button.

Chapter 9

My thoughts raced as I drove out of the hospital parking lot. I wasn't exactly sure what had happened in that hospital room, but I knew two things for certain: one, strong forces of evil were afoot in my neighborhood, and they seemed to emanate from two weird, smelly kids with black eyes; and two, forces of good were also at work, and they were even stronger, especially when wielded by men like Tank.

"I don't get it," Brenda mumbled in the back seat. "If those kids are stealing babies from pregnant women, what did they want with the Hanson kid? Are the two situations even connected? And what has any of this to do with the professor?"

I shook my head and slowed for a red light. "I don't know."

"The situations don't have to be connected," Tank said, rubbing his temple as if he felt the approach of a headache. "Evil goes after innocence. Why would evil beings mess around with people who are already on a road to ruin? Evil wants to destroy the innocent—animals, babies, children. It takes little pleasure in bringing down someone whose life is already ruined."

In the rearview mirror, I saw Brenda glare at Tank. "Feeling a little judgmental, aren't we? Who are you talking about?"

Tank shrugged. "I think you know what I mean. God wants to lift people up, bring them out of addiction, crime, dangerous lifestyles. The forces that oppose God want to bring people down—keep them them addicted, drunk, and sick. Most of all, evil wants to keep people ignorant. They think they're partying and having fun, but all they're doing is setting themselves up for disaster. The man who gets drunk and visits a prostitute while he's out of town—he's destroying his marriage. The college girl who gets drunk at a frat party and ends up getting raped by a group of guys—she ends up with a venereal disease and comes to believe that men can't be trusted. Evil demands a high price. It destroys people."

Brenda crossed her arms and looked out the window, and when I glimpsed the pained look on her face I wondered if Tank's words had awakened some painful memory from her past. We knew each other pretty well, but Brenda had kept a tight grip on some chapters of her history.

"I get what you're saying," I told Tank, "but right

now all I can think about is the professor. If he's not there when we get back, I'm going through his stuff—"

My mouth went dry when my gaze focused on the path beside the road. Walking along the edge of the sidewalk, dangerously close to cars whizzing by, were the two creepy kids. I recognized them instantly, even from the back, because something was obviously *wrong* about them. They walked together, their arms hanging straight down, their heads facing the road ahead, moving like two small automatons with no sense of life about them—

"Hey," Brenda said. "Isn't that—"

"Yes," I answered, stepping on the gas. I sped up and passed the kids, then pulled onto the side of the road and shoved the gearshift into park. Without thinking I opened the door, stepped out, and crossed in front of the vehicle. Upon seeing me the kids stopped and stared. But when Tank stepped out of the car, the kids made a sharp right turn and hurried into an empty lot where weeds grew knee high and broken bottles glimmered among the wild grasses.

I bent and caught Brenda's gaze through the car window. "Keep an eye on Daniel," I warned. Tank's warning about evil and innocence had given me the feeling that Daniel might be in more danger than any of us.

Then I took off after those kids.

With Tank jogging beside me, we tore through the empty field, picking up sand spurs and narrowly avoiding a couple of red ant hills and areas sprinkled with broken glass and rusty debris. I could see the horizontal strip of blue water on the horizon and beneath it, the swaying sprays of the sea oats. The sinister siblings—if that's what they were—were nowhere in sight, but surely they had to be just past the dune that served as a windbreak between the beach and the waterfront houses on this road . . .

Tank and I reached a narrow walkway through the dunes and followed it, reaching the beach at the same time. Breathless, we looked north and south . . . no black-eyed kids in sight.

Lots of people were on the beach—older people, tanned as old leather, reclining on beach towels or reading books beneath umbrellas. Young mothers with their little ones, playing in the wavewash and looking for seashells. Lots of children, lots of innocents, only the active, loud, normal-acting variety.

The BEKs had disappeared again.

I heaved a heavy sigh and crossed my arms. Tank gave me a sympathetic look, then gestured toward the beach. "If you want, I'll walk south a little way to see if I can spot them—"

"They're gone," I said. "They have a way of disappearing when they don't want to be found."

I turned, my heart feeling like lead in my chest, and followed the path we'd created in the tall weeds. "What is this stuff?" Tank asked. "Florida wheat?"

I gave him a smile, but only because I knew he was trying to lighten my mood. "It's just weeds," I said, "but I'd admit it does look a little like wheat—"

I stopped. "Hold up a minute—look how we flattened these weeds when we ran through here. Why didn't the kids leave any kind of trail?"

Tank scratched his head and looked around. The weedy stalks around us stood straight and unbroken, stirring slightly in the wind. I couldn't see any other places where they'd been stomped or broken, except for one small area about twenty feet away.

I walked toward that spot, wondering if the kids could be hiding in the weeds. That'd be a good trick, hiding right in front of us . . .

I caught my breath as we drew closer. The flattened area was circular in shape, reminding me of . . . .

"A crop circle," Tank said, staring at the field with wide eyes. "Just like Brenda's picture."

I quickened my step. Brenda hadn't drawn *just* a crop circle, she'd shown me holding something inside that circle—

I froze when I heard an unexpected sound among the snap and crackle of weeds beneath our footsteps. "Shh," I said, stopping to hold up my hand. "Listen."

I heard it again, a soft mewing sound, almost like a kitten. I rose on tiptoe, trying to see above the line of stalks along the edge of the circle, and what I saw turned my blood cold.

A baby. A pale, motionless infant, still shiny and wet with fluid and a smear of blood.

"Tank, call 911," I told him, my heart rising to my throat. I didn't dare voice my next thought: we might have found Mrs. Diaz's missing baby.

Chapter 10

To my surprise, the baby was still alive.

We followed the ambulance to the hospital, of course, and waited in a lobby while doctors checked the baby to be sure it was healthy and unharmed. I knew they'd also take blood and try to determine whether or not the child belonged to Mrs. Diaz. DNA tests took time, so we wouldn't know anything for certain today, but with every passing moment I felt more certain that we'd found the missing child.

"Yea for us," I murmured under my breath as Tank bought a candy bar from the vending machine.

"We might have found the baby, but I don't have any idea why or how."

Tank grinned and offered me the candy bar. "Sure I can't tempt you?"

"Not right now." I shook my head. "I can't focus on food when I'm upset."

"That's when I find myself craving sweets." Tank fed another handful of quarters into the machine. "I think sugar fuels my brain cells."

I sank into a plastic chair and closed my eyes, forcing myself to think. Where was the professor when we needed him? If he were here, he'd point out some connection I'd missed, something that tied the baby to the kids and that spot on the beach. If those kids had been responsible for taking the baby—somehow—then why had they brought him back? Had they been walking on that road to bait me? Had they purposefully lured me to that beach so I'd find that baby? Unexpectedly decent of them, if that was their intention—at least the infant wouldn't die of dehydration or exposure from the Florida sun.

And how could anyone explain the time factor? That baby was still wet with fluids, but someone had removed it from its mother's womb at least two days before. Of course, the baby could have come from someone else . . , but I doubted it.

"Didn't expect to find you here." I looked up at the sound of a familiar voice. Police office Chad Edwards stood across from me, his notepad in his hand. "The doctor said you were the one to find the baby."

"We found him," I corrected, pointing at Tank. "We saw those odd kids again, and followed them onto the beach. The kids disappeared, but on our walk back to the car we found the baby."

"In the middle of a crop circle," Tank said, narrowly eyeing Edwards. "As strange as that sounds."

"Strange is right," Edwards said, "Considering that no one grows crops along the beach. *Legal* crops, that is."

I smiled at his little joke, knowing that it wasn't uncommon for more daring locals to be busted for growing marijuana plants in their backyards. "Is the baby okay?" I asked.

Edwards nodded. "The doctor said he's in remarkably good condition, considering where you found him. Odd, though—he said the kid was still covered in amniotic fluid, which rules out Mrs. Diaz as the mother. We're treating the case as an abandoned baby."

"I wouldn't—" I hesitated, not wanting to reveal too much about our world of bizarre and impossible situations—"I wouldn't make the usual assumptions in this case. I have a feeling that you may encounter evidence that runs counter to the usual laws of science."

"And reality," Tank added. He gave the cop a deliberate smile. "We could tell you stories you wouldn't believe."

The cop gave us a skeptical look, then leaned against the wall. "The doctor did uncover something unusual in Baby Doe's case. Seems they did a routine scan and found a metallic implant near the base of the child's skull. Would you two happen to know anything about *that*?"

I shivered with a chill that was not from the air. An *implant*?

"What, like a microchip?" Tank asked, eyes wide. "Like a tracking device?"

The cop shrugged. "I don't know what it is, and neither does the doc. He's never seen anything like it."

"Are they gonna take it out?" Tank asked.

The cop pressed his lips together. "Not right now. Something about its position between two nerves— too risky to remove it."

I stood and walked to the candy machine, suddenly possessed of a nervous energy that made me want to run screaming through the halls. Where was the professor? If he were here he would have answers. If he couldn't think of an answer, he'd at least point us in the right direction. He was the calm we depended on, the voice of reason, the one who was never swayed by emotion or whim or—

As if he'd read my mind, the cop tapped my shoulder. "Any word from your missing professor?"

"None."

"Maybe he'll be waiting when you get home. If he is, give us a call, okay? Otherwise, we're sending an officer over. Since your guy's been gone twenty-four hours, you can file an official missing persons report now."

I thanked him, then gestured to Tank. "Let's go find Brenda and Daniel. And let's hope Officer Edwards is right about the professor coming back."

We walked into a quiet house that seemed to be waiting for us. Even Abby, who was waiting for us in the foyer, skipped her usual canine fandango and greeted us with small licks of our hands.

I dropped my house key on the foyer table, then listened for sounds of life. I heard nothing but the slam of car doors outside as Brenda and Daniel brought up the rear. Dust motes danced in a beam of sunlight from the open door, but nothing else moved.

"Professor?" I called out, clinging to the slim hope that he would answer.

No reply.

I knew I ought to go to the professor's room and start looking for clues, but something in me was not at all comfortable with going through his things. We had been good friends, yes, and co-workers, but he had never intruded in my private life and I never wanted to intrude in his. I felt free to go through his professional papers and to open any documents he placed in our shared dropbox, but I would never have dared to snoop among his personal files, paper or digital.

"Anyone hungry?" I asked, heading toward the kitchen. "I could make a bowl of tuna salad, if anyone wants to make a sandwich. There are cold cuts in the fridge, and maybe some hot dogs, if anyone wants to nuke a couple of them . . ."

Brenda made tsking noises with her tongue, her way of rebuking my lack of attention to proper nutrition, but I had more important things on my mind. My boss had gone missing from my home, and I felt personally responsible. Plus, he was *my* boss . . .

I stopped, my hand on the kitchen counter, as a memory suddenly surfaced. That night, after he'd made me promise to print that group selfie, he had kissed me . . . the first and only time he'd ever done so. What was that about? I had assumed he was only feeling nostalgic, but what if he'd known something was about to happen to him? What if he'd been receiving messages or threats, and didn't tell me or the others because he didn't want to worry us?

I turned to Brenda, who was pulling out cheese and mayonnaise out of the fridge. "Has the professor said anything unusual to you lately? Anything about threats or anyone who might want to hurt him?"

Brenda scowled. "Are you kidding? If I knew someone wanted to hurt him, I'd tell them to go for it. Put the man in his place."

I ignored her barb and looked at Tank, who had already taken a seat at the table. "How about you, Tank? Did the professor mention anything odd to you?"

His brow wrinkled, then he shook his head. "I don't understand half of what he says, but none of it seemed any stranger than usual."

I drew a deep breath. "I miss him," I confessed. "It feels strange for us to be together without him. I feel like we're kids bumbling around in confusion because our father's been taken away."

Brenda rolled her eyes. "He ain't no father of mine. And if he decided to walk out on us, that's fine with me. Maybe we can finally get a little peace and quiet around here."

I dropped to one knee so I could look Daniel in the eye. "Little buddy," I said, gripping his hands, "can you see any one else in the room? Anyone besides me and you and Brenda and Tank?"

He lifted his gaze and scanned the space around us, then checked out the corners of the ceiling. "No," he said finally, lowering his gaze to meet mine. "Just us."

"No professor?"

He shook his head as the doorbell rang.

Officer Edwards stood outside, along with a man and woman in plain clothes. "Hey," Edwards said, gesturing to me. "This is Abby Goldstein and these—" he pointed to the people behind him—"are Lewis and Brandolini, crime scene techs. If you could show us to the professor's room . . ."

I nodded and let them in, then led the way to the bedroom the professor had been using. "Everything's just as he left it," I said. "I looked around in here, but didn't want to mess anything up in case—well, you know. So you might find my fingerprints, and my grandparents', but—"

"I doubt we'll be fingerprinting," the woman, Lewis, said, "since this doesn't appear to be a crime scene. We're just going to take a look around and see if we can pick up any ideas about where your professor might have gone."

"I don't think he went anywhere," I insisted. "He's not from this area, so where would he go? He wasn't the type to sit in a bar, and as a recovering alcoholic, he didn't drink. He didn't particularly like the beach—"

"What does he like?" Brandolini asked. "Everybody likes something."

"He likes books." I crossed my arms and nodded toward the stack of books on the desk. "He likes to read. He's super intelligent, so he doesn't do what other people do."

"We'll keep that in mind." Lewis pulled a pair of rubber gloves from her pocket, then drew them on. "We'll call you if we need you."

Taking the hint, I went back to the kitchen.

By the time the police had finished in the professor's room, Brenda, Daniel, Tank, and I had cleared out the kitchen and gone to the living room. Officer Edwards led the two techs down the hallway, then stood by the fireplace and kept his head down as he held a sheet of paper with two fingers.

"I'm glad you're all together," he said, lifting the paper. "I found this document on McKinney's computer and clicked *print*, not sure what would happen. When I heard the sound of printing from the room across the hallway, I realized his laptop had been wirelessly connected."

"Yeah," I said. "I set it up so he could print the speech he gave at UT."

"Anyway—" Officer Edwards looked directly at me— "he addressed this letter to you, Ms. Goldstein, but it's really for everyone. Maybe you should read it."

I tried to stand, but my legs suddenly felt as solid as marshmallows and I sank back into the sofa. Edwards saw my predicament and stepped forward, handing me the note.

I skimmed the heading, saw that the letter had been dated on the day he took our group photo, and began to read:

> Dear friends—
> I have come to feel a profound respect for all of you, even Ms. Barnick, so perhaps you should consider this my tribute to the courage that resides in each of your hearts.
> Tank, you are a prime example of how appearances can be deceiving.

Though you look like an overgrown fireplug and have the intellect of a tree stump, you possess a wisdom not often found in more educated and cultured men. I salute you, sir, and give you my respect. And as to that flaming brightness for which you hold great affection, I must warn you— men have been burned by such passions. Do not be like the man who spent all he had on a treasure he could neither hold nor handle.

Daniel, while I was at first unconvinced that a child could be of any practical use in such a motley crew as ours, I have come to appreciate your gifts and your sense of timing in particular. Furthermore, your attachment to Ms. Barnick has proved useful in that it has shut her mouth on more than one occasion. Good lad. Grow in peace, Daniel, and if it is possible for me to peer through space and time in order to keep tabs on you, know that I will do so.

Brenda, my sharp-tongued, nicotine-stained, misanthropic acquaintance: as much as I hate to admit it, your particular gift has saved my shriveled and cynical behind more than once, so for that I thank you. And if the passing years sprinkle your waspish nature with the proverbial spoonful of sugar, be a dear and dust it off, will you? I cannot imagine you other than you are.

Andrea—first, dear girl, please accept my apology for any worry or trouble this has caused you, especially considering that I am writing this in your home. But though you have never pried or queried, you surely must know that I have made many regrettable choices on my journey along the path of life. I have therefore decided to end this path. I have learned all I need to know.

I digress. So sorry. I am giving my old apartment the boot— key inside ceramic ant. Landlord has been busy traveling so don't expect him to repaint. Rent due on seventh. File speech copy under "dimension," please, for others may wish to read. Remember— unlike me, you never needed help. Godspeed.

I bid all of you a fond farewell.

Sincerely,

James McKinney

I lowered the printed page as the professor's words tumbled and leap-frogged in my head. What was this about? The letter read almost like a last will and testament, but the professor had left us no property, and he certainly hadn't—

"We think James McKinney is dead," Edwards said, locking his hands. "This letter is his suicide note."

Suicide? I blinked at Edwards, then turned to the others. "That's impossible—isn't it?"

Tank grunted. "The professor wouldn't kill himself. He was too smart for that."

"The big guy is right," Brenda said, thrusting out her chin in the professor's defense. "The professor wasn't the type to off himself. No way."

"There's no proof," I pointed out. "And this letter says nothing about killing himself."

Edwards took the letter from my hand. "I have decided to *end this path*," he read. "That's the language of suicide."

"He wasn't the suicidal type," Tank repeated. "No way."

"He was clearly distraught," Edwards said, bracing one arm on the fireplace mantle. "And distraught people often write or say things that don't make much sense. They're confused. They're upset. They ramble, they put down words that don't fit and they don't care. After all, they're set on checking out."

"But how would he do that?" I challenged. "There's no body. No blood. No empty pill bottle."

"There's an ocean." The female crime tech pointed to the water beyond the sliding doors. "All he had to do was walk across the beach, enter the water, and swim toward the horizon. Eventually he would have gotten tired and drowned."

"But the body—"

"Will wash up eventually . . . or not." Edwards clamped his lips together. "I hate to be indelicate, but sometimes the body is devoured by predators."

I lowered my head as a vein began to throb near my temple. None of this could be happening. Nothing made sense to me, and though I was usually quick to spot a pattern in any series of events, numbers, or diagrams, I couldn't see any pattern in the past few days.

"Thank you," I said, my voice hoarse. "If . . . you find anything—"

"If we have any news, we'll be sure to call or come by," Officer Edwards said, his face grim. "And I'm very sorry for your loss." He looked around the group. "I'm very sorry for all of you."

ANGELA HUNT

Chapter 11

After the cops left, I went outside and sat on the deck. The usual ocean breeze had turned into a real wind, rising the edge of an approaching thunderstorm. Dark clouds loomed over the gulf, and the wind pushed at my cheeks as if urging me to go inside.

Fat chance. I wasn't ready to face the others.

As the professor's assistant, I felt a mantle of responsibility hovering over my shoulders, and I wasn't ready to be the leader, the hostess, or anything else I was expected to be. All I wanted was time alone to sit and feel whatever it was I had to feel once my emotions sorted themselves out.

We were all struggling to deal with our emotions. Brenda had gone immediately to her room, and soon the sounds of cursing and crashing objects came through the door. Of course she would be angry— she had only begun to open that steel door around her heart, but with this loss, she'd probably slam it shut again.

I had worried about Daniel—he didn't respond well when stressed, and I had no idea how he would react to the news that the professor would no longer be with us. But after the police left, Daniel got up and went into the professor's bedroom. I followed, curious about what he might want, and watched from the doorway as Daniel ran his hand over the desk, the laptop, the notebooks, even the professor's pajamas and suitcase. Finally he moved to the nightstand, where he ran his hand over McKinney's phone and watch.

Daniel picked up the watch and turned to look at me, a question in his eyes. "Yes," I said. "You can have it."

I helped him put strap it on his slender wrist, then watched as Daniel went back down the hallway, his right hand holding the bulky watch securely on his left wrist.

We all mourned in different ways.

I heard the rumble of the sliding doors behind me, but didn't turn to see who was coming out. Maybe if I stayed quiet, the intruder would realize that I didn't want company.

I brushed the wetness off my cheeks and turned my head toward the south, then heard a heavy creak of a board behind me. Only Tank was heavy enough to creak boards like that.

Next thing I knew he was sitting beside me. I looked at him, about to tell him I wanted to be by myself for a while, but he spoke first: "A person shouldn't have to cry alone."

"No, no—I'm okay. Really. You don't have to babysit me."

"I wasn't talking about you."

And then, while I watched in total astonishment, Tank covered his face with his hands and went completely to pieces.

We wept together, of course—the big lug in my arms and I in his. And when we had cried long enough for the clouds to start weeping in sympathy, we got up and walked onto the beach, both of us ignoring the rain that felt like cold needles on our faces.

I kept asking myself why the professor's death affected me so deeply. I had never been in love with him, so it wasn't like he was my one great passion, but I admired and respected him deeply. I also—though he would not have wanted to hear this—pitied him in many ways. He could be charming, warm, loving, and paternal, but few people ever saw those traits because he hid them beneath a mantle woven of bitterness and cynicism.

I couldn't stand thinking of him in the past tense.

Tank was no longer crying, but those broad shoulders were slumped beneath the weight of grief he carried. We were all feeling the loss, and if we stayed together, we'd feel it for years to come. The professor's absence would be visible every time we sat at the dining table and every time we rode in a car. No one would sit in his favorite chair when we gathered in my grandparents' living room, and we still tiptoed past the bedroom he'd used out of respect for the hours he spent studying there.

Officer Edwards clearly agreed with the crime techs; the professor had committed suicide. He must have seen me punch in the security alarm code, so after kissing me goodnight, while I was in the shower or noisily brushing my teeth, he had disarmed the system, then re-armed it again, taking advantage of the thirty-second window in which he could open a door and slip out without sounding the alarm. According to the Officer Edwards's theory, the professor had been walking across these sands as I got ready for bed, and he had been swimming for Mexico by the time I fell asleep.

He would have been dead by the time I woke the next morning.

Even though the logical part of my brain understood that scenario and even appreciated that the professor hadn't killed himself in my grandparents' house, something else in me refused to accept that idea. Reason protested that James McKinney was about as likely to kill himself as he was to sprout a fish's tail. Impossible. Unlikely. Categorically out of the question.

"Umm." Tank paused as if he were fishing for words. "What do we do now?"

I shrugged and blinked up at the rain. "Beats me."

"Do you think we'll keep going . . . as a group, I mean? Whoever's been sending us plane tickets and invitations, do you think they'll keep doing it?"

"I don't know, Tank. I don't know any more than

you do." My words came out harsher than I'd intended, and my conscience smacked me when I saw the hurt on Tank's face. "Listen." I turned and took his hands. "I'm sorry. But I'm as confused as you, maybe even more. I've not only lost my boss, I've lost . . . who I am. I was his assistant, his right hand, and I could have kept being his right hand forever. Now I don't know what I'm going to do for a job, for a career, for . . . anything."

My voice broke. I started to turn away, but Tank drew me close and patted my back, like a daddy comforting a little girl. "It's gonna be okay, Andi," he said, his voice a reassuring growl in my ear. "Though what the cops said made no sense, I guess maybe suicide never makes much sense. No matter how well you think you know a person, nobody can ever really know what's going on inside someone else's head—"

"But I *did* know," I insisted, pulling away. "I knew him better than anyone! I knew he was fixated on his studies into other dimensions, that he was all excited about that presentation. He kept saying that if we could find a way to bend time, we could go back and repair all the damage we'd done in our past, that we could start over. He wasn't finished with his work, but our encounters with those different universes had given him new ideas and he was just beginning a new phase of—"

I halted as a sharp shard of memory sliced into my thoughts. *I have made many regrettable choices on my journey along the path of life. I have therefore decided to end this path.*

What if the professor hadn't been writing about suicide at all?

"Holy cats." I pulled away from Tank and ran for the house.

Chapter 12

"Andi, what *are* you doing?"

"I think—" I pressed my hands to the side of my head in an effort to still my spinning thoughts. "I think he was talking about dimensions, not death. He wanted to end a third-dimension path, that's all. Where's that darn letter?"

Brenda dropped her magazine and searched the room, then pointed to the coffee table. I snatched the letter up and reread the so-called suicide note. No doubt, the letter had been written in the professor's language and style, all except the ending—

"Here." I took the letter and sat at my grandmother's desk, then pulled a highlighter from the drawer. "This paragraph, the one where he talks about his apartment. Notice how it doesn't flow like the rest of the paragraphs?"

Tank peered over my left shoulder as Brenda looked over my right. "Yeah, so? The cop said the professor was losing it at that point."

I snickered. "Have you ever seen the professor lose it? Ever?"

The corner of Brenda's mouth dipped. "Good point."

"It's gotta be a message. Something . . . encrypted. A pattern."

I stared at the page, highlighter in hand, then focused on the paragraphs addressed to me.

> Andrea—first, dear girl, please accept my apology for any worry or trouble this has caused you, especially considering that I am writing this in your home. But though you have never pried or queried, you surely must know that I have made many regrettable choices on my journey along the path of life. I have therefore decided to end this path. I have learned all I need to know.
>
> I digress. So sorry. I am giving my old apartment the boot— key inside ceramic ant. Landlord has been busy traveling so don't expect him to repaint. Rent due on seventh. File speech copy under "dimension,"

please, for others may wish to read.
Remember— unlike me, you never
needed help. Godspeed.

"By the way," Brenda drawled, "I can't say that I was pleased to read his comments about me. Even a man who's planning to check out should have better manners."

"He *wants* people to think this is a suicide note," I said. "Because . . ." I waited for an answer to pop into my head.

"Because why?" Brenda asked.

I sighed. "I got nothin'."

"What's that about a ceramic ant?" Tank said, pointing to the paragraph that was nothing like the others. "Some kind of garden statue?"

"He's not a gardener," I said, focusing on that line. "And his landlord isn't a person, it's the university. And he doesn't pay rent, the apartment is faculty housing, provided for tenured professors in residence . . ." I caught my breath. "That entire paragraph is bogus, but no one who reads this letter would know that except . . . me."

"So—" Brenda twirled one of her dreadlocks around her finger—"what's he trying to tell you?"

I grinned as the light came on. "It's a code, probably a numbered sequence. So what number would he use?"

We looked at each other. "The year?" Brenda suggested.

"His birthday?" Tank said.

"It's gotta be a smallish number," I said, reading the paragraph again. "A number small enough to repeat in this paragraph."

"Five." Daniel appeared beside Brenda. He lifted his hand and counted, pointing to each of us: "One, two, three, four, and—" he pointed to the letter— "five."

"Five of us—makes as much sense as anything. So I'm keeping every fifth word, starting with my name."

> Andrea ~~first, dear girl, please~~ accept ~~my apology for any~~ worry ~~or trouble this has~~ caused ~~you. But though you~~ have ~~never pried or queried,~~ you ~~surely must know that~~ I ~~have made many regrettable~~ choices ~~on my journey along~~ the ~~path of life. I~~ have ~~therefore decided to end~~ this ~~path~~.

"Andrea accept worry caused have you I choices the have this," Brenda read. "Makes no sense at all."

"So let's try the second paragraph."

> I ~~digress. So sorry. I~~ am ~~giving my old apartment~~ the ~~boot— key inside ceramic~~ ant. ~~Landlord has been busy~~ traveling ~~so don't expect him~~ to ~~repaint. Rent due on~~ seventh. ~~File speech copy under~~ "dimension," ~~please, for others may~~ wish ~~to read. Remember— unlike~~ me, ~~you never needed help.~~ Godspeed.

"I am the ant," Tank read, "traveling to seventh dimension wish me Godspeed." He blinked. "That doesn't make any sense, either."

"Oh, yes it does." I brought my hand to my mouth as the pieces fell into place. "The ant, remember? The sugar ant from his speech, the ant traveling on the thin piece of paper. If you twist the paper, the ant can move from one dimension to another. The professor—somehow—found a way to move into the seventh dimension!"

"Wish me Godspeed," Brenda whispered, her eyes widening. "How in the world did the old fart manage to do that?"

"I don't know," I answered, laughter rising from my throat, "and no one is going to believe us if we try to tell them where he is. But he's not dead. He has only . . . moved."

Tank stepped backward and rubbed his brow. "I still don't get it."

"You don't have to." I threw him a reassuring smile. "You know how Littlefoot came from another universe? It's kind of like that. The professor's just gonna be out of touch for a while."

"But everyone's going to think he's dead," Brenda pointed out. "And face it, maybe he is. Maybe his technique or whatever he used to zap himself out of here didn't work. Maybe he got to the seventh dimension and a monster ate him. Maybe he transported himself to a Flatland kind of world where he doesn't fit, so he imploded. So many things could have gone wrong—"

"Maybe it doesn't matter," I said. "All of that stuff is out of our control, even out of *his* control. But at least we know he's not floating out in the Gulf. He's not being eaten by sharks. He's . . . he's like an explorer in the new world, conquering unexplored territories."

"He wanted to correct his mistakes," Tank said, his eyes softening. "I get that. And if he can find a way to do that—" Tank shrugged. "I'd love to hear all about it sometime."

"So what do we do now?" Brenda asked. She glanced toward the hallway, where the empty bedroom lay. "The man ain't comin' back."

"I guess—" I made a face—"as distasteful as it will be, I guess we have to go along with the suicide scenario. That's how the professor set it up, so I guess that's what he wanted."

"Roger that," Tank said.

"Okay," Brenda echoed.

Chapter 13

As the black-clad mourners milled around the empty coffin, I lifted my gaze to the low-hanging clouds and wondered if the professor had found a way to peel back the curtain and spy on his former dimension. Probably not, considering it had taken him a lifetime to figure out how to engineer a path to wherever he was now.

He would have been pleased by the turnout at his graveside. Lots of faculty, the university president, and dozens of students who had either loved his lectures or hated them, depending on their point of view. Someone in his family had sprung for an expensive spray of roses on the casket, but no other flowers stood at the graveside. As per the wishes expressed in the professor's will, there had been no funeral or memorial service. There would be no wake, but I knew that most of the university faculty would soon head over to the Thirsty Scholar Pub, where they'd lift a glass in his memory.

I stood in respectful silence as the funeral director murmured a respectful, "Ashes to ashes, dust to dust," and the casket lowered into the grave, accompanied by the whine of an electric motor. A couple of mourners tossed carnations into the dark space, then most people wandered away.

I remained, feeling it my duty to see this charade through to the end.

I wasn't the only one who lingered. A woman in a black hat and veil stood on the other side of the open grave. She pressed a tissue to her eyes, and sniffed as she wiped away tears.

Who was she, and where had she been during the professor's final years? She must have loved him, because her tears were genuine . . .

I stepped closer so I might better see her. Silver hair brushed her shoulders, and when she lifted her head I saw a lovely face marked by the passing of more than a few years. She might have been the professor's age, or even a little younger, and she was still a beautiful woman. Was she one of the professor's regrets? Had he found a way back to her . . . and his younger self?

I was working up the courage to speak to her when the grave diggers approached. One of them lowered his shovel and nodded at me, then he and his partner removed the fake grass that served to disguise the mound of dirt that would fill in the grave. Time to go.

I drew a deep breath and looked up, but the woman had already left the graveside. I saw her walking, not toward the parking lot, but another section of the cemetery. Did she know someone else buried here?

I strode forward, intending to hurry and catch her, but turned my ankle when I stepped in a patch of soft dirt. "Ooof!" I sank to the ground as gracefully as I could, and the grave diggers dropped their shovels and hurried to help.

"Gotta be careful around here, Miss."

"Watch your step." Crooked smile. "We wouldn't want you to fall in."

I managed a smile in return. "It's these heels. I don't usually wear shoes this high."

I brushed dirt off my knees and tucked my purse under my arm, intent on catching the dark figure moving through the tombstones and mausoleums.

"Ma'am?" I called, hobbling forward. My ankle was beginning to throb, and if I pushed it, I wouldn't be able to walk tomorrow. I stopped and pulled off my shoes, then hop-skipped forward, lurching left to right as I searched for the woman in black.

I stopped and waved one of my shoes. "Hey, lady!"

She turned and looked at me, and the expression on her face was so heart-rending that I nearly wept. My mind had supplied a hundred reasons why she would be standing at the professor's grave—she was a former lover, a long-lost sister, an ex-wife, a fellow teacher, a nun he'd known in his days as a priest—and she had loved him, but time and circumstance had kept them apart. But now she'd come here to mourn him—

"Will you wait, please?"

The woman didn't answer, but moved behind a wall of marble that blocked my view.

I hurried on. Finally I reached the spot where the woman had disappeared, but when I looked around, I saw nothing but a marble tombstone etched with:

Marissa Lorena Longworth,
1958-1999
She walks in beauty.

No sign of the woman. Only a fence at the eastern boundary of the cemetery and a path that led back to the entrance.

I followed the path, taking my time and placing as little weight on my injured ankle as I could. When I got back to my apartment, I'd put my leg up, cover the ankle with a bag of ice, and call Tank and Brenda. They had wanted to fly up for the graveside service, but I had talked them out of it, promising a full postmortem report.

Knowing that I had my hands full with cleaning out the professor's apartment and office, Tank had volunteered to be my go-to guy for reports on BEKs. He had set up a Google search, and was trolling the Internet for new reports of BEK sightings—which, he told me unhappily—were on the rise. Black-eyed kids were being reported in every country, on every continent. A guard at an Arctic outpost had even opened his door one night to find two black-eyed kids outside.

At least the Diaz family had their baby again. Though, according to my grandmother's latest report, the doctors had not yet been able to remove the mysterious implant.

I got to my car, leaned heavily on the back passenger door, and managed to get my door unlocked and opened. Thankfully, I didn't have to use my injured ankle to drive, so I slid in, carefully placed my left leg in a safe position, and pulled my car door closed.

And then, in the side view mirror, I saw the professor, as clear as stark reality. I turned, expecting to see him standing beside the car, but I was alone. I looked at the mirror again. The professor still flickered there, then he pulled something from a coat he wore and held it up—the printed photo, the selfie of our group.

My smile cracked into a sob. The professor's smile softened, then he pressed the photo to his chest and covered it with his hand.

And then he was gone.

Caught in a place between laughter and tears, I leaned my head against the steering wheel and struggled to get a grip on my emotions. He was alive. He was okay. He was just . . . somewhere else.

I smiled as I slid the key into the ignition.

SNEAK PEEK AT HARBINGERS 12:

THE VILLAGE

ALTON GANSKY

In the Blue Ridge Mountains of North Carolina, tucked away in the dogwood and hickory trees and bordering a noisy creek, is a town——a village, really. It is hidden from the world and unknown to even longtime residents of the area. Tourists who show up there are usually lost and residents of the town are happy to show them the way out.

I've been there and I don't much wanna go back. Neither do my friends. There isn't much to catch the eye in Newland. Not on the surface, anyway. Just some old buildings on Main Street, a shop or two or three geared to the needs of the residents, not passersby or interlopers like us. There are two eating establishments serving up grits, fried trout, and biscuits with gravy. There is a saloon for those who prefer to drink their nourishment from a beer mug, and a sheriff's office that is open most Tuesdays. The GONE FISHIN' sign hangs in the window the rest of the week. There is a small, white chapel at the end of the street for God—fearing men like me.

Newland is two towns, not one. I mean that literally. I know it makes no sense but it is still true. Those who have followed our previous adventures know that very little of what we face makes sense.

Not to me, anyway, and the others don't seem to know any more than I do. This might be the weirdest story yet. Only the good Lord knows if stranger things await.

My name is Bjorn Christensen but you can call me Tank. Everyone else does. And now, I have a story to tell you. I don't expect you to believe it. I lived it and I have trouble believing it. Still, it happened, and it happened in this way . . .

Don't miss the other books in the Harbingers series which can be purchased separately or in collections:

CYCLE ONE: INVITATION
The Call
The House
The Sentinels
The Girl

CYCLE TWO: MOSAIC
The Revealing
Infestation

Infiltration
The Fog

CYCLE THREE (in progress)
Leviathan
The Mind Pirates
Hybrids
The Village

SELECTED BOOKS BY ANGELA HUNT

Roanoke
Jamestown
Hartford
Rehoboth
Charles Towne
Magdalene
The Novelist
Uncharted
The Awakening
The Debt
The Elevator
The Face
Let Darkness Come
Unspoken
The Justice
The Note
The Immortal
The Truth Teller
The Silver Sword

The Golden Cross
The Velvet Shadow
The Emerald Isle
Dreamers
Brothers
Journey
Doesn't She Look Natural?
She Always Wore Red
She's In a Better Place
Five Miles South of Peculiar
The Fine Art of Insincerity
The Offering
Esther: Royal Beauty
Bathsheba: Reluctant Beauty
RISEN

Web page: www.angelahuntbooks.com

Facebook: https://www.facebook.com/angela.e.hunt

CPSIA information can be obtained at www.ICGtesting.com
Printed in the USA
LVOW10s2158240816

501735LV00014B/288/P